BIG PIG

To my favourite farmers, Philip and Hilary
~ M.D.

For all my great nephews and nieces, and as ever
my wonderful wife, Tiziana
~ J.B-B.

SIMON AND SCHUSTER
First published in Great Britain in 2005 by Simon & Schuster UK Ltd
Africa House, 64-78 Kingsway, London WC2B 6AH

Text copyright © 2005 Malachy Doyle
Illustrations copyright © 2005 John Bendall-Brunello

The right of Malachy Doyle and John Bendall-Brunello to be identified
as the author and illustrator of this work has been asserted by them in accordance
with the Copyright, Designs and Patents Act, 1988

Book designed by Genevieve Webster
The text for this book is set in Adobe Garamond
The illustrations are rendered in watercolour and crayon

A CIP catalogue record for this book is available from the British Library upon request

ISBN 0-689-87484-7
Printed in China
1 3 5 7 9 10 8 6 4 2

BIG PIG

Malachy Doyle

John Bendall-Brunello

SIMON AND SCHUSTER
London New York Sydney

"It's time to go, Pig," said John Henry,
but the pig wouldn't go.
"I'm sorry," said John Henry,
"but big pigs have to go."

"I brought you in when you were born –
your mummy couldn't feed you.
But now it's time to live outside,
for that's what big pigs do."

"You'll like it," said John Henry.
"It's a cosy little pighouse."
So he picked him up and carried him,
across the muddy yard.

But Big Pig didn't like it.
He was cold and he was lonely,

so he upped and he waddled back home.

"Come on, then," said John Henry.
"I've a palace for a pig!"
So he popped him in the barrow
and he wheeled him down the lane.

But Big Pig didn't like it.
He was cold and he was lonely,
couldn't bear it on his own,

and so he upped and he waddled back home.

"All right, Pig," said John Henry,
"you can stay here for tonight.
But you'll have to go tomorrow,
for that's what big pigs do!"

When morning came
he heaved him into the basket of his bike,
and he cycled to another farm,
a very special piggy farm,
a long way away.

"You'll like it," said John Henry.
"And I'm sure that you'll be happy."
Then he climbed back on his bike,
and off he cycled.

But it was late and it was dark,
and he could hardly see a thing.
He rode into a wood,
and then he bumped into a tree,
and then he fell into a hole,
and he was stuck, completely stuck.

"I'm lost," cried John Henry.

"And I'm hungry and I'm tired!

It's dark," cried John Henry, "and I'm frightened!"

"Who's that?" cried John Henry.

"Who's there?" cried John Henry.

"Oh help!" cried John Henry. "Oh no!"

"It's my pig!" cried John Henry.
"It's my lovely smelly pig!
Take me home!" cried John Henry.
"Lead me home!"

So Big Pig plodded
homeward,

with John Henry close behind,

and they staggered,

and they waddled,

and they trudged back to the farmhouse.

"You saved me!" cried John Henry.
"Now you can stay with me forever!"
"Grrr…unt," said Big Pig.
"Grunt, grunt."